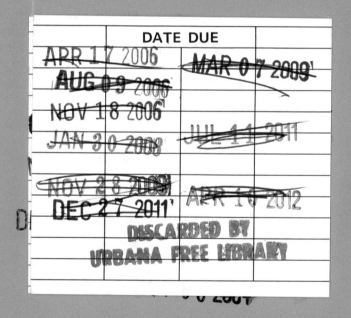

Red Moon Follows Truck

For Karen, Georgia and Natalie.
S.E.H.

For Stefan, dog's best friend,
in memory of Florence.
L.E.W.

_____

Text copyright © 2001 Stephen Eaton Hume
Illustrations copyright © 2001 Leslie Elizabeth Watts

National Library of Canada cataloguing in publication data
Hume, Stephen, 1947–
Red moon follows truck

ISBN 1-55143-218-8

1. Canada — Description and travel — Juvenile fiction. I. Watts, Leslie Elizabeth, 1961– II. Title.
PS8565.U556R42 2001   jC813'.54   C2001-910577-0   PZ7.H89Re 2001

First published in the United States, 2001

Library of Congress Catalog Card Number:
2001089939

Orca Book Publishers gratefully acknowledges the support of our publishing programs provided by the following agencies: the Department of Canadian Heritage, The Canada Council for the Arts, and the British Columbia Arts Council.

Design by Christine Toller
Printed and bound in Hong Kong

IN CANADA
Orca Book Publishers
PO Box 5626, Station B
Victoria, BC Canada
V8R 6S4

IN THE US
Orca Book Publishers
PO Box 468
Custer, WA USA
98240-0468

03 02 01 • 5 4 3 2 1

Red Moon Follows Truck

written by *Stephen Eaton Hume*

illustrated by *Leslie Elizabeth Watts*

ORCA BOOK PUBLISHERS

We live on a blueberry hill.
We love it here.
But Mom says we have to move out west.

My dog Gypsy wants to know: How far is west?
As far as the earth to the moon?

I think moving makes her sad.
Let me hold you. Good dog.

She wants to know why we're moving.
Questions, questions!
We're moving because Mom and Dad have a new job.
They're both carpenters.
They're going to build boats in a town by the sea.

Gypsy, now do you understand?

We pack our pickup truck with all the important things: chocolate chip cookies, dog biscuits, a cedar box filled with fishing gear, two bamboo fishing poles, sleeping bags, a tent.
We squeeze into the truck and Dad says, "Let's go!"

Goodbye, blueberry hill.

We drive and drive.
One day we camp in the woods.
Around midnight a little bat flies inside
the tent and gives us a terrible fright!

Gypsy, quiet please.
It's only your guardian angel checking to see
how you are.
Now go back to sleep, okay?

Another night we camp out again.
Snow starts to fall!
Gypsy is tired of camping.
She wants to stay in a hotel.

It's the biggest snowstorm I've ever seen.
The tent shakes in the wind.
Gypsy crawls into my sleeping bag
and chases rabbits in her dreams.

In the morning we drive to a fancy hotel.
No dogs allowed? That's so unfair.
Dad sneaks Gypsy in under a big wool blanket.
"It's our dirty laundry," he says to the hotel man.
That night I hardly sleep at all. The radiator clangs
like a bell all night.

We wake up early and eat breakfast in bed.
Gypsy has toast and jam.
She slurps the whipped cream from my cup.
Then she asks for more.
Hush, now. Laundry isn't supposed to bark.

We're back in the truck. It's quiet on the road.
I sing all the cowboy songs I know:
"I'm So Lonesome I Could Cry,"
and about a hundred more.

We drive into the night.
Dad says, "Look!" A big red moon is trailing after
the truck.

We keep rolling west. The highway flies by.
It doesn't snow anymore. It rains. It thunders.
Hailstones drop from the sky.
I lose count of the days.
We camp under the stars and leave the truck radio on.
Mom and Dad dance to cowboy songs.
Gypsy growls while jackrabbits play in the dark.

One day, late in the afternoon, we stop in the
mountains and go fishing for rainbow trout.
I slip on the rocks and fall in the river.
My bamboo pole goes sailing over a waterfall.

Gypsy jumps in to save me, but she disappears
over the waterfall too. Dad picks me up and
carries me to shore on his back.

I am shivering.
Where is Gypsy?
She's nowhere to be seen.
I look north, east, west and south.
I almost start to cry.
Then I see her climbing
up the riverbank
with my fishing pole
in her mouth.

We build a fire and dry my clothes.
Gypsy lies down with her nose between her paws.
We set up our tent by the river and get ready for bed.

Mom kisses me goodnight and tucks me in.
"Know how the moon seems to follow the truck?"
she says. "Like the moon, our love is with you
wherever you go."

I lie awake and listen to the river.
The big red moon is shining above me.

In the morning we get in the truck and start driving again.
Gypsy leans out of the window, her face to the wind.
Maybe she can tell we're almost there.
Maybe she can smell the salty air.

I know we're getting closer because we don't stop.
We drive through the night, over mountains, past
towns and cities and moonlit farms.
I go to sleep with Gypsy in my arms.

When I wake up in the truck we're crossing
a bridge over the Pacific Ocean.

I have never seen water look so blue.

That night I go to bed in our new house by the sea.
The big red moon is shining in my window.

Gypsy, are you happy?

Yes, me too.